I0618243

Killing the
Bogeyman
I & II

Peter J. Michael

Killing the Bogeyman I & II

ISBN-13: 978-0-6459234-0-7

Published by Peter J. Michael

ALL BOOKS BY THIS AUTHOR ARE:

THE GREAT WAR AGAINST TERRORISM

KILLING THE BOGEYMAN I & II

SUMMARY

New York City was overtaken by scourge and pestilence.
The upright citizens of the city were aching for change and strong leadership to clean up the streets and offer them true protection.
They looked only to one man to become their weapon of war; their hammer to crush and destroy all those responsible for putting their lives in harm's way!

The vermin and filth of the city wanted to burn New York into the ground.
They resented the new Mayor of the city.
They wanted payback against his ideology.
They figured that they set up a death trap for him.
But the real question was who set who up …
for death that is?

Contents

Killing the Bogeyman I & II

KILLING THE BOGEYMAN

The head is weak.
The heart is sick.
They have no souls.
They are cowards.
These are the scum of humanity.

Why should we spend money to keep
these filthy evildoers alive in prison?
They should be killed.
They should be sent to the death penalty!

Rapists, murderers, drug pushers – all
such scumbags have no rights to live.

The law must be fixed.
The law will be fixed.
I will fix the law.

Why will I fix it?
It's very simple.
I am the LAW!
It will be done.

Those menaces of society who do not deserve to live will not live.
I am the LAW.
It will be done.

Should we heal the evil so they can recover and commit more evil?
They deserve to suffer every human condition nature has bestowed upon man and woman.
The evil deserves it a thousand-fold.
And then some.
And then some more.
Never stopping to dish out misery upon misery, curse upon curse, excruciating suffering upon excruciating suffering, with an infinite surplus of destruction against each and every one of these evil disasters who have cursed our society with their detestable beings.
They should not be healed.
Never!
Never!
And never again...!

The mean-spirited deserve no compassion, no mercy, and no opportunity for reprieve.
No.

It will be ruthlessness for ruthlessness.

We will humble the pride of the arrogant of spirit.

We will crush their bones.
We will shock their hearts.
I will break them mentally and crush them spiritually.

And physically, when they realise the law finally works against them, they will be forced to endure every medical condition imaginable by the stress I will cause them.

They will suffer fevers, wasting diseases, hunger, thirst, bites from large creatures.
They will choke from polluted air.
As they have poisoned the fabric of our society, so too will their entire beings become tainted by all that surrounds them.

As they have killed their victims, so too shall they be killed in like fashion.

Those who contaminate society with their evil pestilence will be contaminated and isolated…until they die!

It will be death for death.
Destruction for destruction.
Suffering for suffering.
Poison for poison!

And they will die.

Why will they die?
It is very simple.
Because I have deemed it to be so.
I have willed it.
I have justified it.
I am the LAW!
It will be done!

Should killers of humanity be given any
rights to live?
Should pretenders and liars be given any
second chances?
No.
These people smile to your face, pretend
to be your friend, and behind your back they
plan to have you ambushed.
Such offenders must be punished with
equal justice.
They kill, so too must these offenders be
killed.

It makes no sense for these evildoers to keep living only so they can create further harm and destruction to the whole world around them.
No.
No sense at all.

It serves no purpose to be lenient to such people.

We must treat the hostile with utter hostility.
We must treat the unmerciful without a shred of mercy.

The evil are only in existence to be made tools for target practise by the righteous.
They are on earth for us to master our use in all forms of self-defence and combat.
We must use them as instruments and objects to become perfect in shooting our weapons, in drawing our swords, in striking them with our hands and feet, knees and elbows.
They must be made an example of what happens when anyone threatens the security of our city, state and territory.
Anyone who threatens the security of our nation must be destroyed.

We must sing in celebration for the new LAWS passed in our governments, which will help us thrive and triumph against our oppressors.

The sinful and contaminators of the human spirit will be thrown onto the electric chair.
They will not be given chances to hinder our efforts through time-consuming legal appeals upon appeals, that only work to cause delay upon delay to their inevitable fate and destinies which await them.

The LAW will become our shield, our protection, strength and salvation against the evildoers of our society.

We must celebrate the ease of the enemy's swift removal from our midst.

As the new sworn in Mayor of New York City, with legislative powers and influence over governments, I am a man of combat, a believer in using war against our opponents to clean our streets from the bloodshed they exact against us, unjustifiably.

The evil opposition and his henchmen
we will throw into our jail cells.
And their punishments will equal their
great abominations.
It will be like-for-like.
Mutiny-for-mutiny.
Pain-for-pain.
Only justice in its purest forms will
suffice when all other watered-down acts of
aggression have failed in the past.

Any law-enforcement officer who fears
to use his weapon against the enemy will be
removed from our police forces.

The enemy, who threatens the lives of
people with a gun, will be showered with our
bullets.
The enemy will be given no chance to
fire his gun, his rifle, or draw his knife on any
mass groups.
For our allies will be better trained, more
resilient than ever, with might, power, and the
strength of the LAW behind his and her every
action of combat and retaliation against our
enemies, who threaten our society with any
forms of terrorist acts.

With our right hands and with our left,
we will strike and overpower the enemy.
We will shatter his spirit.
We will curse his existence.
We will blast him to pieces with our
powerful arsenal.

We are the greatest of the great when it
comes to matters of security.
We are majestic in our actions and in our
deeds against the enemy.
We are holy.
We are strong and powerful.
As opposed to the enemy, who is sick,
evil, cowardly and weak against us.
The righteous will steamroll the
unrighteous.
The great will cause the wicked to
tumble and fall into their bitter graves.

The enemies will feel the firm power of
our blasts against him and her.
The evildoers' arrogant audacities will
become humbled at the great and powerful
impact of our targeted attacks and fury against
them.
We will consume, crush and destroy the
opposition with wit, skill, powerful ferocity and
poetic justice.

We will blast these evildoers clean off
the face of our earth and straight into hell.
For their demises must be incorporated
sooner rather than later.

Why postpone the inevitable of the
enemies' destructions?
Why indeed?
It serves no purpose to anyone.

The wicked will feel the blasts of our
weaponry bombarding them, until their entire
existences become heaps of skeletal wreckages.

We will shock their minds and their
hearts with our powerful retaliations against
them.

The evildoers' think they are all high and
mighty in their presumed untouchable wicked
ways.
But they are incorrect.
They are all guilty of self-delusions.
We will prove the filthy and the unclean
completely wrong.

We will pursue the wicked until they
tremble in fright with the might of our
adversity against them.

We will crush and destroy the root of all evil in our lands, who will meet destruction upon destruction, together with all their chief advisers, henchmen and criminal officers and aiders and abetters who assist them, to cause insecurity in our much esteemed to be, secure lands and territories.

We will takeover the evildoers' empires and dismantle their wicked evil kingdoms - and send such kingpins and all their fiery serpent aiders and helpers and henchmen to destruction all at the same time.

We will draw our weapons and aim them at these wicked people - and we will not falter or fail in our goal to destroy the enemy completely with our guns and with our hands.

Mark my words: the enemy will be enemies no longer.
Because they will be given no more chances to attack us or any righteous member of our community ever again!

We will divide these evildoers and conquer them.
We will dismantle and squash their empires with unequalled resilience.

We will dry up all their sources of income to drive them and their ambitions into the ground, with no money, no affordability for manpower and no hope to ever pose a threat to us ever again.

We will blow the wicked evildoers' empires and their people to the next world, with no halting or swaying from our ambitions to exterminate them completely and absolutely.

We will cut off the enemies' heads like the snakes in the grass they are.
They are wicked, they are powerless against us.

We will win because we are the greatest.
We are majestic in our authority against the opponent.
We are righteous and holy in our actions and holy in our deeds!
We will shoot our weapons at the wicked until they fall onto the ground and the earth swallows them up.
It can be no other way!

The righteous are society's guide and with my absolute mandate in office by the people of the community, I will become the ultimate Leader of Justice!

I was voted in office by the righteous members of the community.
And the righteous were all victims to the wicked.
The righteous that thirsted for justice.
The righteous who knew me by name and by nature.
The righteous who gave me the absolute mandate, the power, and the supreme authority to do whatever it takes to make their community safe!

And I have heard the cries and pleas of the righteous ones against the wicked.
I know that the wicked have made them tremble even in their own homes.
For as long as the wicked are among us righteous men and women, no abode is safe.
No building or house can be called a safe haven.
No.
All people of all races and creeds are at risk of being molested by such fiery creatures within our midst.

But I have heard the begging of the people.
And fear not O righteous ones.
Fear not any longer.
For I have heard you.
The difference you all seek will come to pass.
It will be made.
The blood of the righteous will cease to be spilled.
But from this day forward let me promise you all: only one group will have its blood shed.
It will no longer be the Good Samaritan.
But it will be the blood of the wicked whose blood will be spilled before you all, you victims of such tragic and terrible abuse.

And the righteous will rejoice at the blood of the wicked being spilled before their eyes and their nostrils, to celebrate the triumph in what will be, the scent of death being unleashed upon the wicked and all its unholy henchmen who support such abominations they commit.

Yes.
The wicked will be forced to tremble when their corrupt lives become ceased.

They will be forced to surrender themselves and their aiders to their diabolical causes.

Their homes and kingdoms will be blown-up and forced to crash onto the ground in pieces – and finally burnt to ashes.

Horror, terror, regret and dread will suddenly consume them.

They will feel the great arm of the law crashing down upon them like a concrete tunnel collapsing onto their skulls.

They will be ambushed as they plan to ambush.

They will be struck with weaponry as they plan to strike unmercifully.

And they will be destroyed as they heartlessly and callously plan to destroy the lifeblood of our great land.

The evil think they are immortal.
HUH!
They are in for a bitter blow, a terrible shock to their systems.

Everything they own…

Everything they amassed to bring about their wealth will be thrown onto the ground in fiery ash.

They will lose everything.

And only the righteous ones will triumph.
The righteous will be glorified by the deaths and destructions of the unglorified wicked enemies.
For the fiery serpent will be sent into the flames.
He and his unholy kingdom that has polluted and terrified our society will be forced to cease-to-exist completely.

I have received the great mandate by the people of this community to deliver them out of slavery from the wicked.
I hereby declare that there will be no more thefts.
No more robberies.
No more rapes.
No more murders.
No more threats and intimidation.
No more stealing one's belongings through murder of the owner preceding the act of theft.
There will be no more committing heinous crimes by anyone and using scapegoats to cover-up the crimes of the real perpetrator.
There will be no acts of perjury and lies under oath in a court of law which attempts to pervert fair justice.

15

There will be no more illegal drug
peddling.
There will be no more illegal acts of any
sort.
For anyone and everyone who breaches
my laws, will surely and swiftly incur the
ultimate penalties' imaginable.
That means equal justice matching the
crime committed.

Anyone who wants to kill, expect to die!
Anyone who wants to steal and commit
robbery and make up falsehoods against
someone to any law-enforcement official in
order to settle a score in a perverse manner -
will have the same punishment thrown in his or
her face as he or she intended to throw at their
intended victim unjustly.
The guilty perpetrator can expect to have
no rights for freedom.

Remember this O fiendish one;
If you go against my decrees and
endanger anyone's life;
If you mock my just laws and official
sanctions;
If you threaten the security of my city,
state and territory in any way, I will come down
on you like the plague enters the flesh of man.

You sinful perpetrator and perpetrators will experience the true meaning of the word 'panic'.

You will suffer unbearable anguish.

You will be struck with excruciating destruction of spirit.

Your minds will suddenly begin to lose its faculties.

You will not know if you are coming or going.

You will wish for a place of salvation, but there will not be one safe haven on earth to find anywhere to escape from my prying eyes into your sick lunatic activities.

You will wish that New York City was not a target for your habitat and crimes.

I will personally strike you with great blows on your head and on your knees.

I will embarrass you in front of your wife, your mistress and/or your girlfriend.

Your own families will become embarrassed by your very existences.

Those who were most loyal to you will prove their sudden unfaithfulness.

Those who called you family will suddenly disown you.

All your wealth and possessions will be seized and confiscated - and instead, distributed to your victims and your victims' families.

Your riches will turn to poverty.
Your friends will become foes.
Your wives and mistresses will have no choice but to enter another man's arms.
Your children will desert you.
You will have no more money to afford corrupt counsel.
You will be forced to enter my courtroom with a lawyer that I will appoint to you.
And that lawyer will be forced to have your worst interests at heart.
He will advise you to accept the worst possible outcome that the justice system will surely bestow upon you.
And you will do so with an anguished spirit.
I will be the one and only cause of your great anguish.
You will become mentally confused.
You will surely not know the difference between good advice and bad advice.
You will not know the difference between good counsel and bad counsel.
Those you think you can trust will be the most treacherous toward you and behind your back.
And your mind will be so confused and disorientated by your sudden declining life

circumstances, that you will surely not have the will to fight back.

And this will all eventuate, because all your allies from your previous life will be forced to desert you.

All your financial wealth you had accumulated from your wicked life of crime you will have lost.

And because you lost your wealth, you cannot buy proper counsel any longer.

But you will be forced to settle for the inconvenience upon inconveniences I will throw in your face.

Your eyes will look at those around you, but you will be unable to see the truth of their motivations where you are concerned!

Are they friend or are they foe?

You will never know.

As you have ambushed others, you will not be able to guess who has been sent to ambush you for your belongings.

Your unsettled and anxious state of mind will leave your judgement severely lacking.

You will think you might have a chance, but the truth is you have no chance at all for anything positive to eventuate in your suddenly rapidly declining life circumstances.

Are you heading for a glimmer of hope
or a sure-fire trap I have set-up for you?
How will you know?
You cannot possibly know.
Your confused and perturbed mind has
left you making one bad judgement call after
another.
And I will confront you.
You will be forced to look into my eyes
as I reveal to you, that I was the one who
changed the course of your life for the worst in
one heartbeat.
With my brutally cold stare into your sick
eyes, you will suddenly know the truth.
I will reveal it to you.
I will force you to understand everything
before I strike you down with the law, MY
LAW.

Just when you thought everything was
OK in your world, I will surprise you with my
own furious and top-secret ambush I had
waiting for you all along, in a time when indeed
you thought all was right in your life.
But I will prove to you that your
judgement was folly once again.
I will show you that nothing was ever
right in your world.

Because your world was built on shaky
ground from the very beginning.
And I will strike you in a time when you
least expect it.
You will surely reap what you sow.
You will surely suffer a thousand-fold
what you caused all your victims to suffer in
their totality.
And all those who are your enemies who
despise you as I despise you, will be let loose to
torment you and mock you wherever you are in
your sudden state of downfall.
And believe one thing if not anything
else: you will lack even one ounce of power to
fight back one iota the severe and brutal
damage I will cause you.
Such irreparable damage.
I will make you lose everything that meant
anything to you in your former life.
That is what I will do to anyone who
breaches my laws - and causes a threat to my
secure and safety decrees bestowed for the
benefit of the good soul citizens of my city and
state of New York, which I serve as its Mayor.

You wicked ones thought you were all-so
powerful and all-consuming.
But I will force you to realise the errors
of your hideous ways.

I will force you to realise the truth of the matter in startling fashion when I impose upon you harsh penalties - and strike you with severe punishments for your wicked and evil ways.

Anyone who defiles my city, to which I am in charge of, will wish that they never entered New York City soil.

It will be blood-for-blood.

I will shed your blood.

There will be no pity, no compassion and absolutely no mercy for any wicked one of you!

You will be destroyed.

I will make you perish!

Just try and provoke me to anger you fiendish derelicts and I will unleash the demons of hell upon you.

You will understand the ruthless power of my retaliation against you.

A retaliation that will be forever kindled, until the earth consumes the very bones of your dead corpses laid onto the very ground and soil that you have once contaminated with your filthy pestilence.

I will mount disasters after disasters upon you.

I will heap ruin upon ruin into your life and the kingdoms you have amassed from your greedy criminal ways.

You will grind your teeth in anguish and despair until the enamel will wear thin.

You will eat your finger-and-toe nails in nervous fear of what punishment you will endure at my hands.

I will set fire on everything you own.

I will make sure that all your enemies inherit your wealth and belongings.

And before your life is ended, you will not have what you don't deserve: that one last meal.

You will die hungry and thirsty.

I want you to think of me and my name and face before you die.

I want you to hate me as much as I hate you O wicked ones of the earth!

You people are so stupid.

You are incapable of learning the difference between right and wrong.

You are too weak to act accordingly.

You are too dim-witted to understand anything.

Your lives are forfeited!

I will cut you all to pieces.

I will blot out your names from all records of human history.

The evil, wicked and ruthless will amount to zero.

The righteous will only prosper!
I will see to that.
I am the LAW!

All of you wicked ones never tell the
truth.
You were born dirty rotten lying
scoundrels.
Anyone who listens to you, believes you
or trusts one word you say is a fool.
You know nothing but treachery.
Your tongues utter nothing correct, just
falsehoods.
You are even deceivers of yourselves.
Is it no wonder why I will relish
punishing you all to the fullest extent of my
new laws decreed!
Every man and every woman who
speaks words of goodness will take pleasure in
your onslaught, you evildoers.

You sinful people never listened to the
pleas of your victims.
So do not cry to me on the day of your
judgements, because I too will not listen to you.
I will only execute your punishments,
with the sole intents to hear you bark like the
crazy mad dogs that you are on the days of your
ultimate punishments.

You will remember that.
You will remember me with every
torture imposed on you all, forever and ever!
You evildoers have committed gruesome
vile acts.
You have no rights to live!
This is the year that your punishments
begin!
It is the year 1992 and in the month of
March that my ultimate position and power has
been established.
This is the new age of reckoning for you
wicked ones.
From this moment on, expect only one
thing to enter your repulsive lives: disaster!
You unrighteous people are a stain to
our city's population.
I do not accept you.
I reject your wicked lives!
I will punish your abominations.
You will die!
And anyone who follows your sick and
corrupt paths will also meet the same equal
measurement of destruction: DEATH!

You wicked ones will all suffer the evil
of your ways.
You enjoy stealing, killing, raping,
betraying.

I will steal your very lives from under
your feet.
So, prearrange your funerals.
Get your caskets ready.
I will throw your dead corpses inside
your coffins, you walking abominations.
You are all lunatics.
And my mind is filled with lunacy and
wild thoughts at the pleasurable prospect of
watching your deaths unfold!
Your whole lives are based on sick-
minded delusions, wasteful fantasies, mass
killings, dread and fraud, you evildoers.
And as you have lived the life of the
fraud, plying your fraudulent trades on others,
and defrauding them, so too shall your true
names on your caskets be thus embedded: that
is, the fraud!
Your iniquities are dreadful!
Your abominations are plentiful!
And your severe punishments will be
eternal!

Punishment upon punishment awaits all
those who put their trust in the wicked, the
sinful, the liars, the weak and the treacherous.
All those who follow the paths of the
evil are not righteous, they are unholy.
They must be condemned, rightly so!

So, behold wicked ones: I will bring a shout of justice to every righteous soul that walks the streets of my city.
And the shouts of justice will be by the very cause, the very justifiable acts to your terminations, you slimy transgressors and abominators of all just laws.

Terror is waiting for you evildoers!
I am your terror, your horror, your curse and your justice!
I know where you are.
I am hunting you all down!
I am waiting for you to rear your ugly heads from the holes in the muddy ground you crawl out of to prey on innocent flesh.
But justice will be forthcoming.
Justice is greater than your evil abominations.
Justice will triumph.
The law will prevail.
And your deaths are inevitable!

I will turn your weapons of destruction against you, evildoers.
With strong arms and an unwavering spirit, and a totally focused mind, I will fight you all until your ends are met.

27

Yes.

I will be your ends, wicked ones!

I will be the face that haunts you in your
nightmares.

But unlike in your dreams, where
shadows are cast - in reality - you will know
who I am.

You will also know that I am coming for
you with much artillery at my disposal, to send
every dirty one of you into the ground where
you will be forced to befriend the worms, the
insects and the filth below that will become
your new home.

That will be your eternal punishments
wicked ones.

You will feel my great anger, my
unquenched fury, wrath and terrible vengeance
to be delivered against all of you evildoers.

I will attack you from all sides.

I will go through all of you like a
tornado!

It will be your lives for all the lives you
took.

And let me enforce my omens of truth:
when I strike you down with my vengeful
wrath, there will be no mercy, no compassion
and absolutely no regrets when I bury you all!

So don't plot or plan any further dreams
of delusions for power.

Because I am besieging your fortresses'
walls and I am closing in on you, waiting in
anticipation to get my hands around your
throats and wring the life out of you, you
diabolical threats to humanity!
So get ready all of you lawbreakers.
You will die a great death of utter misery,
despair and unimaginable suffering for the evil
sins you have committed.
Your power structures will remain no
longer.
Everything you have is disintegrating
before your very eyes.
I am going to burn your evil empires
down with fire!

You evildoers have polluted my lands
with your abominations.
You have caused terrible grievances on
all who mistakenly come in contact with you -
and those you intentionally come in contact
with.
You are a curse to all of humanity.
You are robbers of all that is holy.
You attempted to monopolise all
industries via your evil.
You wanted to control everything, thus
forcing your competition into bankruptcy.

But you will not get away with your
attempts to drive my city into the abyss socially,
politically or economically, via the endless job
losses your delusions of monopoly on all
business endeavours would thus create.
You are thieves!
You are frauds!
You are sick and crazy fanciful schemers!
But get ready you lawbreakers: I am
going to hang you all with every scheme you
concoct in your very sick and foolish minds.
You are all ungodly, overrun by evil.
I am going to bring destruction to both
you and the invisible evil force that resides in
your black souls, lurking among all of you
cursed seeds of humanity.
My wrath against you all will never
waver, falter or diminish in the midst of the
bloody war I have waged against you evildoers!

So stop being proud of yourselves, you
sadistic schemers;
You have nothing to be proud of.
All your hands and feet are dirty.
You have committed atrocities, you devil
worshippers.
I will be the end of your pride and
shameful arrogance, you evildoers.

You think you will enter my city and
stain it with your immoralities.
You will experience much anguish from
my revenge against you.
According to your sick actions, you will
all face not just the same measure of
punishments, but even much greater.
I will paralyse you all with terror.
I am your terror, your horror, the very
authority that will end your disgraceful lives!
Your abominations have defiled my city
with the blood you have shed on countless
innocent lives.
You accept bribes in order to kill, maim
and destroy the innocent.
You make profit by murder and
extortion.
You even steal from the poor and the
needy.
You oppress everyone with your
pestilence, you sinful curses of humanity.
You burst out of your fortress hideouts
only to pollute the lands.
You trouble all of whom you come in
contact with.
You are poison to democracy.
You thrive on violence.
Your feet foul everything, all the lands it
touches.

You thrive on corrupt dictatorship.
But I have a trap set-up for all of you.
You will all fall right into it.
Then I will cast you out and fling you
into my jail cell where you will await your
much-deserved punishments!
Not one of you will escape!

The only way to cleanse this city's lands
is by tearing you down, you evildoers, and
removing you all from
circulation…permanently.
You evil fools will suffer my great
indignation.
I will pour my powerful wrath upon you
all.
I will never end my vengeance against
you until I have consumed every maggot one of
you!
And then you swine will know that I am
the LAW!

So forget about going to church and
confessing your sins to a priest, wicked ones.
It will be useless for you all.
You are all beyond redemption.
No righteous spiritual force listens to
prayers of the damned, the deceived and the
ungodly.

If a priest tells you otherwise, he is lying
to those gullible enough to believe his anti-
spiritual fibs and deceptions!

You evil suckers of our society are
burdens to all that is pure.
And the only way to deal with burdens is
through sheer force of will, without any
compassion.
You evil walking calamities will not
profit from your corruptive trades any longer.
But you will become cursed from my
lands – and only a memory to the rest of my
city's population who will just simply look
down on you all with shame.
After I finish with all you evil sinners,
you will be nothing but a bad memory.
You will be something to be cursed at
and looked upon with scorn.
Your guilt is great and the wounds I
inflict upon you will be incurable, remember
that O wicked ones.
So look at your feet, you repulsive
lawbreakers;
You evil rebellious people to just laws,
look down at yourselves, where you are headed.
You are swiftly and surely sinking into
the mud.

And as I watch all you evildoers sink, I
will be very satisfied with myself.
I will take great pleasure in watching
misery upon misery striking every wicked
person within my midst.
It will make me feel glad.
My spirit will be uplifted enormously
beyond imagination.
Yes.
I rebuke you, wicked ones.
Blood, death and destruction shall fall
upon you all.
I am Robert Stewart.
I am the new Mayor of New York City.
I have spoken.
What I have decreed will come to pass.
The righteous will no longer suffer the
tyranny of evil men.
Tyranny in all its twisted forms ends
NOW!
It will be done.
I am the LAW!

KILLING THE BOGEYMAN II

So the trap was elaborately set.
The cheese was planted, so to speak.
Now the rats were crawling out of their holes.
They were falling for the rat trap, hook, line,
and sinker.

I had a census of every person who resided in
the city of New York.
I had the names of every citizen.
The good, the bad and the ugly.
It was my job to get inside their skulls and see
what was going on in there!
In the case of the bad and the ugly, I studied
the crap that made up the very sick dimensions
of their mad minds.

I knew what they were planning.
They were all up to no good.
It was always the case.
When one scumbag dies, another always takes
his place.
That was why the task of law enforcement
would never cease-to-exist.

When all else may liquidate and fall apart at the seams, the work of a police officer would always be in demand.
When one gangster was caught, imprisoned and/or killed, another sicko entered the city to take his place.

And now I had swift elaborate surveillance planted on all my targets.
There were masses of them.
They entered New York for one distinct purpose: they planned to burn the entire state into the ground – and bury every innocent civilian beneath the remaining ash.

I, as the new Mayor of the city, already serving six months so far to date, took pride in publicly declaring a zero tolerance for all crimes, including Mob activities.

The new breed of gangsters who entered New York wanted to exploit that.
They began to band together for one purpose: power.
And to achieve that endgame of power in their very diabolical minds, meant one other fundamental aspect: to exact bloodshed on a grand scale.
It was mass murder they planned.

We had criminals coming into New York from all ends of the globe.
From all countries.
They thought that since I, the New Mayor, had declared a cease-to-exist policy on all underworld activities in the city, that their actions would then become unapprehended.
They considered that I would not expect anyone to breach my rules.
They thought I would not be prepared for those rebellious transgressors to my necessary severe decrees put in place, to safeguard all the innocent of the entire state of New York.

But the new breed of major underworld criminals entered New York City under false pretences, assuming new identities and phony credentials matching those fake names.

Some entered New York as benefactors to the poor and the needy.
Some entered New York as pastors of the church.
And some claimed to be political candidates to serve the community.

But political candidates they were surely not.
They were in fact political terrorists.

They formed unholy alliances together.
Upon arrival into the city, they recently
arranged a supposed top-secret meeting in
Manhattan, inside one of their front-owned
casinos in that borough, to discuss their
diabolical plans.
The new breed of criminal gangs and Mafia
chiefs then concocted scheme after scheme
after scheme, which would indeed burn New
York City into the ground.
They planned to kill a great many casualties
along the way.

They wanted control of the police departments.
They wanted control of the churches.
They wanted complete political power which
would spread nationwide.

But more than anything, they wanted the Mayor
of the city of New York to be executed.

And with psychotic glee, they joined hands and
began singing a diabolical hymn that went as
follows: 'Let's kill the Mayor, let's kill the
Mayor – and may no man conspire again to
bring such allies of our world asunder!'

These criminal chiefs then brought together in one room claimed that the New York City Mayor was too dangerous to them and their livelihoods.
They insisted that the Mayor stood in the way of their power structures to control all aspects of the city: from political power, to all major industries and manufacturing companies, even tobacco.

They wanted the political power to ban tobacco use from all legitimate means of sale in New York, so they could profit from its availability only through the yet-not-vanquished, but-still-thriving Black Market, to then be distributed to the consumer.

And they planned to kill the Mayor and all his do-gooder police who stood in the way to thwart their criminal plan and plans.

They wanted control of the shipping industry on all New York City ports.
They wanted ownership of the entire state's waterfront area and customs personnel, to secure the safe smuggling of their illegal import-export trade to all foreign and domestic markets.

These new criminal regimes plotted and planned to overthrow and contradict the new Mayor's entire policy agenda and political structures, in which I had set-up, to safeguard the city from criminal control.

The new underworld sharks who entered the city in droves, wanted to control the entire state.

They were even planning to kidnap and threaten, at random, hand-picked women off the street, innocent passersby – and force them to work as paid sex workers inside their illegal prostitution rings.
They would secretly film the sexual acts discreetly of the sex workers and their clients inside private rooms - and sell the films to overseas buyers and suppliers of erotic movies.

They wanted to use women in New York City and profit from them as they were forced to work as prostitutes, selling their bodies without consent.

And one of the women targeted was the Mayor's daughter.
My daughter.

They wanted to assassinate me and then use my own daughter as a prostitute to supposedly rub it in my face, even from Six Feet Under, as they planned.

These dirty scumbag rat bastard freaks would stoop to new lows.

They wanted to infiltrate the police departments.
They wanted to infiltrate City Hall.
They wanted to infiltrate the churches – and even use the church as a safe haven for drug distribution, and a place to conceal their illegal arms and drug merchandise - and to stash their dirty money-laundering profits inside.

These were the discussions that took place during their not-so-secret meeting.
These were the discussions I had discreetly recorded.

I had pinpointed every criminal who entered the city.
I had initiated very strict and quite elaborate surveillance on all the major criminals in question.

It was my job to become much better organised
than organised crime officials.
And anything less, meant the deaths of all
innocent civilians in my state, on my watch, in
which I was paid to protect.
There was no room for failure in this.
Absolutely no room for failure whatsoever.
We had to nail them.
We had to bury these fiendish scums.
We had to destroy them.
Or they would destroy us.
There was no other way.

So we watched.
And we waited.
And we listened from a secure safe distance to
the horrible revelations, mad crosstalk and
seriously chaotic conspiracies thus planned, by
the new gangsters who entered the city with a
very hideous agenda.

The products of their discussions were not only
horrendous in nature, but they were also quite
revealing, in a no-holds-barred sadistic type of
fashion.

They were quite forthright in their disclosures
amongst themselves.
They had no shame.

These were the products of their evil words and
sick conspiracies:

First, we kill the Mayor – and then New York
City is ours.
We will control the entire state.
The Mayor has very bad ideas that contradict
ours.
He is a menace to us.
We need to stop him.
We need to humiliate him.
We must kill him.

Perhaps we can plant a bomb inside the driver's
seat headrest of the Mayor's car where he sits
inside - and blow his head off.
Or perhaps we can have someone to approach
the door of his home as a deliverer or
something;
It doesn't really matter if it is conducted during
the day or night.
And when the Mayor answers the front door of
his home, we can have him greeted by a man
holding a machine gun to blow him away to
hell in many pieces.
Perhaps we can plant a bomb inside City Hall
and kill him right along with all his pest
colleagues and associates.

We can also plant poison gas fumes to pollute the air vents of his home and his office at City Hall.
We can take him out-this annoying enemy of ours, by putting poison inside the Main Water Supply that he drinks from.

I know a lot of you here prefer VX (nerve agent).
But this week, my poison of choice happens to be Botulinum toxin.

But at the time of his death, we must not only kill his people at the same time;
But his family must also be killed.

All his family.
All his children.
His wife.
His parents.
His brother.
His sister.
But we only keep his daughter alive.
She will make us a fortune.
Indeed.
I believe she will become very lucrative for us.
We can profit from her assets.
We will force her to become our number one call girl.

Without big daddy around to protect her, she
will succumb to our demands, one way or
another.
She will have no choice but to obey us.
She will obey us completely.

In fact, the entire city will obey us.
All of New York will fall under our mercy and
absolute control.

And that is only the beginning.
Because today we will control New York;
Tomorrow, our plans will expand nationwide.
And we will not stop until the lifeblood of
America is circulating inside the palms of our
very hands.

And once we control the entire US, then the
day after, we look to own the entire world.
We will take over all large corporations globally.
We will execute everyone who doesn't belong
to us.
We will kill off all minds not in sink with our
ideology.

We will become the sole financial currency in
which everyone else around the world depends
on for survival.

There can be no other life allowed to survive without our permission.

And then...then, we must constantly pay our dearly departed Mayor homage.

Yes.
That foolishly heroic Mayor wants to, in his own words, 'Stop all crimes!'
What a dreamer!
And that man of dreams thinks we are crazy!
That ridiculous unattainable goal in itself should have him committed to some insane asylum.
Not us.
But he-that damn Mayor should be put into the nuthouse.

He wants a city without crime.
Well.
It will be a pleasure to disappoint him.

He wants to create a peaceful and harmonious atmosphere for the people of New York.
It will truly be our pleasure to make it as noisy as hell.

The Mayor wants to bring us all to his beloved electric chair.

We will be glad to disappoint him again and
again and again.

Let us slag on his silly dreams.
Let us forever ridicule his anti-crime policies.

He wants to play Robin Hood with our
fortunes.
He wants to take our wealth away from us, and
instead, distribute it to the poor, the
impoverished and the homeless.

Now, as payback, we will use his own daughter
for our profit and gain, when we force a gun to
her head, and make her a sex slave to our client
drug dealers and their cliental.

So may we never forget the dreadful Mayor of
New York City.
Even as he lays waste into the ground, we must
never forget his laughable and quite delusional
antagonistic dreams against us.
May we never forget to mock his silly ideology
which opposes our very own.
And may we never forget to plant fresh roses
on his tombstone – and remind his turning
soul, that such roses were bought from the
profits provided to us via his daughter's new

career, thus being forced to perform it to perfection.

So salute, New York Mayor.
Your end is near.
Your death is imminent.
Your last hurrah is now!

Let us kill him.
Let us inflict pain on all his family.
Let us destroy all those who honour that bastard's name.

As he wants to open a grave for us, we instead must throw him inside.
As he wants to humiliate us, we must quickly prove ourselves the better enemy – and first humiliate him.

You vocalised your hatred for us Mayor, so arrogantly.
You were foolishly loud in your plans against us.
You revealed your hand too readily and too publicly.
And now it is you who will fall, not us.
It is you Mayor who will fall, with every self-righteous indignant shout and scream you gave in hatred of our world.

Yes.
Our world which is in direct opposition to
your so-called do-gooder values.
But the do-gooder doesn't last in this world,
Mayor.
Only the bad evil guy prevails.
Only the wicked prosper.
The good guy, as they say, dies young.
And you will be living proof to that certifiable
truth and documented philosophy, O Mayor.

We look forward to shutting for good, that
bloody loud trap of yours, you call a mouth.
We will cancel your words of condemnation
against us.
We will overturn your false sense of triumph
you think you have against us.

You hate us, do you Mayor!
You want us to prearrange our funerals, isn't
that what you so brazenly said.
You wanted to send us to our deaths hungry
and thirsty.
Well, now it is payback, O nasty Mayor.
Now we look forward to punishing you, in your
own words, 'like-for-like'.
It will be 'mutiny-for-mutiny', as you so
eloquently put it, dear Mayor.

We want to hear you scream Mayor, in
excruciating pain.
We want to inflict upon you the very same
tortures you wanted imposed upon us, with
such horrendous words of bravado you
directed our way.

You will lose, Mayor.
You will lose everything, dear Mayor.

You will lose your autonomy.
You will lose your self-respect.
You will lose your powers and strengths.
You will lose your family.
You will lose your unashamed pride.
You will lose it all.
And most of all, you will lose your life.

So hear us now O Mayor.
We are coming for you.
We are going to send this city and state of yours
into the great depths below.
We will transform it.

You wanted peace.
We will give you war.
You wanted our deaths.
We will overthrow you and instead, you and
your world will crumble and die at our hands;

The hands of your opponents.
You are finished Mayor.
You will be only but a memory.

Your arrogant words driven against us so
foolishly publicly have angered us all.
And we will take heed of your words.
But we will seek retribution against you, dear
Mayor.
We want to cut you in pieces and send them to
your mother's and father's dinner table.
We want to make an example of you, Mayor.
We don't like your words of hatred for us.
You have upset us, Mayor.
You have angered us, Mayor.
We want blood for that, Mayor.
Your blood.
You will not shed our blood, but yours will be
made to flow out from your body like a river.
We will drown your offspring with your blood,
dear Mayor.
So get ready to receive your last rites.
On second thoughts, we will deny you all
permissions.
You will be denied any assistance in your final
hour.
We will torture you.
We will butcher you.
We will massacre you.

And on the day of your massacre, we will sing
the following words: 'You are dead, you are
dead, let there be no one like you to replace you
who is sick in the head'.
Does that rhyme, O arrogant Mayor?
Do you like that song, O pompous arse of a
Mayor?
Does that anger you enough to swell the veins
in your head, O irritating Mayor?
What do you think of that, O Mayor?

Are you listening, you insufferable self-
righteous Mayor?
What do you think of our rejoicing your
demise, dear Mayor?

Come on, give us some feedback.

We want to know if we are irritating you, O
Mayor.
Are you pissed off with us, Mayor?
Come on, show yourself Mayor.
Fall into our trap instead of trying to lead us to
a trap.
Just die, Mayor.
You arrogant sod, just die!
Make that one last hurrah!
Make us happy.

Make us laugh by just dying, Mayor.

We want to see you dead.
We want to see those close to you dead.
We want all those in your world burnt at the
stake.

You will not burn us.
We will burn you, Mayor.

You think you will burn down our empires?
You foolish arrogant sod of a Mayor, listen up!
You approach us with a match.
But we approach you with dynamite.
Our bombs are greater than your fire.
Our words are stronger than your mental
ravings.
Our armies are better disciplined than your
police forces.

We will win.
You will lose.
We will laugh.
You will cry.
We will live.
And you will die.

So say goodnight, dear Mayor.

For the rest of us will rise to sing good
morning.
But you shall not.

You will not starve us.
We will starve you.
You will not crush us.
We will crush you.

You say you hate us.
Well, dear Mayor, we don't like you either.

You want to choke us with polluted air.
We will choke you with every arrogant self-
righteous word of doom and gloom you throw
our way, O you menace of a Mayor.

You walk with your head held high like you are
better than us.
But does your shit smell better than ours, O
Mayor?
Look into our eyes as you answer that, O you
rascal of a Mayor.

O smarty-pants Mr. Mayor.
You are such a smart aleck.

You are rude.
You are crude.

You are crass.
You are brass.

You are shrewd.
You are cunning.
You are vulgar.
You are unashamedly brazen.

You constantly boast of your infinite
achievements.
You possess infinite ambition.
But prospering against us you will not.
You will see.
You will see the light, Mr. Arrogant Mayor.

You will not win.
You will not have the last laugh against us.
You will not have the last hurrah!
Your plans to muddy the waters under our feet
will fail.
Yes.

Let us bring death to the Mayor.
Let us bring death to his allies.
Let us bring death to his family.
Let us bring death to everyone who loves this
pompous Mayor.
If one person loves him, we will kill that
person.

If the entire city loves him, then we will kill the entire population of New York.

Today.
Yes, today.
Dear Mayor;
Today;
You die!

So get a priest ready.
Your funeral is soon!
By day's end, you die!
You and all those around you are dead.
Hear us, Mayor.
Dead;
DEAD!
DEAD!

****

And that was it.
I, the Mayor of New York City, just heard
about enough of this horse manure-spouting
moronic dickhead words, from the gutter traps
of humanity's low-class delinquent race.

I was to prove the real purpose of my verbal
explosions against the scum of this city.

They thought my taunts were instead crazy
ramblings.
Perhaps the products of some hubris or
misguided miscalculation on my part.
Perhaps they thought both.
But these idiots were true numbskull insults to
the human race.
They were surely mistakes of creation.

My public loud derisions directed at this filth
and human trash of society had a purpose.
It was indeed to taunt and thus lure the rats out
into the open.

They were not setting a trap for me.
I planted the seeds of my harsh words to in fact
plant a trap for the scum of humanity, as those
were in question.

My menacing words served a distinct purpose.

My words served a great purpose.

It was the **TRAP** I set up for these arseholes and creeps.

My words were intended to anger them.
My words were intended to needle them.
My words were intended to have them all come after me.

And it worked!

I, the Mayor, set myself up as bait in order to flush out everyone's true motivations out into the open.
My words had exposed every dirty seed that resided in my city and state of New York.

It was I who set the trap for them, whilst those stupid idiots thought my words were putting myself into a spider web trap.
But they were wrong!
My strategy worked!

Now I got them!

I got them all recorded on hidden surveillance equipment, confessing their schemes and revealing their plans and conspiracies.

So I, the Mayor of the city, led my standby, heavily-armed police troops, who were planted all the while in close proximity, to now close in on the targets.

We burst open the two doors of the large casino office situated on two opposite sides. We then cornered the underworld goons planted inside.
And with much anticipation and proven success to my endgame strategy, via previous taunts given, much to the enemies' dislikes, the trap of casting them all together in one place was an effective strategy tool indeed!

I, the Mayor of New York City, gave the order to the heavily armed police troops, to open fire their weapons against all the threats to them and society as a whole!

Our presence was certainly unexpected by all our targets.
And just as the enemies' jaws dropped down in comically emotional surprise and shock, I became satisfied.
I assisted my police troops.

Holding my own large weapon, all of us lawmen and lawwomen witnessed the justifiable cutting down of the enemies in magnificent form.
We all fired our weapons simultaneously.
And we witnessed the flesh of the enemies being pierced with our bullets from head to toe.
I wanted it that way!
I wanted these enemies to be made a true example of what happens when any unrighteous wicked element dares to enter my city – and attempts to mock my laws and challenge me to a duel.

And so I fired my weapon with brutal intensity.
The cavalry fired their weapons with the same powerful determination and calibre.
It was truly a wonderful sight seeing the filth and the trash of humanity get their just deserts.
Could there possibly be anything finer in this life, than watching your worst enemy and enemies being brought down to their bloody weakened knees?
Perhaps there was.
But right now my mind and thoughts were solely concentrated on the magnificent sight before me.

The flesh of the enemies was being torn apart from their bodies, limb from limb, everywhere.
We witnessed the gruesome bloodbath unfolding before our eyes.
The enemies' bones were being broken in numerous pieces by the seemingly endless firing of bullets from our artillery.
We just didn't want to stop firing at all.
We couldn't stop.
It didn't matter how dead the enemy and enemies were.
It was as if our hatred and loathing for them, wanted to just never stop blasting them all straight to hell.
If only we could bring them back to life in order to kill them again.
That was the product of our true emotions for such a hideous group of individuals, as they were.

And within moments, the screams upon screams being sounded by the fallen bad guys had come to an abrupt halt.

The bad guys had all dropped like dominoes onto the hard parquetry floor of the large casino office.

Forty-six heinous murderers and organised
crime chiefs had at that moment plunged to
their agonising deaths.
And, in addition, with the targets' bodyguards,
that tally of those terminated, amounted to
much, much higher in number.

I predicted that the wicked would not escape
justice in all its true forms;
Poetic justice.
I predicted that the wicked and the immoral
would not live in my city.
I predicted correctly that the unrighteous would
surely and swiftly die under my watch!
And that is what I, Robert Stewart, Mayor of
New York City prophesied.
And so as I had decreed such necessary deaths
of the immoral to eventuate;
So such deaths were carried out to perfection,
with absolutely no hesitation whatsoever!